THE INCREDIBLE ADVENTURES OF

MARY JANE MOSQUITO

a one-woman musical in one act

with book, lyrics, and music written by

Tomson Highway

Illustrated by Sue Todd

FIFTH
HOUSE

Published in Canada by Fifth House Limited, 195 Allstate Parkway, Markham, ON L3R 4T8
Published in the United States in 2016 by Fifth House Limited, 311 Washington Street,
Brighton, Massachusetts 02135

Fifth House acknowledges with thanks the financial support of the
Government of Canada for our publishing activities, and the Ontario Arts Council
for their support of our publishing program.

Library and Archives Canada Cataloguing in Publication
Highway, Tomson, 1951-, author
Mary Jane Mosquito / Tomson Highway, Sue Todd.
– First edition.

A play.
ISBN 978-1-927083-38-3 (hardcover)
I. Todd, Sue, author II. Title.

PS8565.I433M27 2016   C812'.54   C2016-903080-6

Publisher Cataloging-in-Publication Data (U.S.)
Highway, Tomson, 1951-, author. Todd, Sue, illustrator.
Mary Jane Mosquito / author, Tomson Highway ; illustrator, Sue Todd.

Markham, Ontario : Fifth House Limited, 2016.
"Mary Jane, a mosquito without wings [who is] mocked by other insects,
discovers her true voice through singing" –

ISBN 978-1-927083-38-3 (hardcover)
LCSH: Canadian drama – 21st century. | BISAC: DRAMA / Canadian.
LCC PR9196.62H544 |DDC 812.6 – dc23

Managing Editor: Kathryn Cole
Illustration: Sue Todd
Text and cover design: Kerry Designs

Printed in Canada

This play is dedicated to disabled children everywhere.

Because they make our world a special place to live in.

ACKNOWLEDGEMENTS

John Miller and Stratford Summer Music,
Andrey Tarasiuk, Claude Labine, Ross Murray, Tom Osborne,
Patricia Cano, Therese Lalonde

CREDITS

"The Incredible Adventures of Mary Jane Mosquito" was a commission from John Miller
and Stratford Summer Music and had its world premiere there, at the musical festival known
as Stratford Music in Stratford, Ontario, on August 9th, 2001
with the involvement of the following artists and personnel:

Mary Jane Mosquito – Patricia Cano
Samba Cheese Sans-facon (i.e. the pianist) – Tomson Highway
Directed by – Tom Osborne
Musical direction by – Tomson Highway
Costumes by – Patricia Cano
Produced by – John Miller and Stratford Summer Music

Book, lyrics, and music written by Tomson Highway.

THE INCREDIBLE ADVENTURES OF MARY JANE MOSQUITO

PLACE:
opens in whatever town or city the show is playing and then reverts
to Petit Petit Le Paw, a tiny suburb of a small town in north-central Manitoba,
then Winnipeg, then back to the town or city where the story started.

TIME:
from late summer 2001 to spring 2013.

DRAMATIS PERSONAE:
Mary Jane Mosquito, a girl-mosquito without wings,
in fact, the only mosquito in the history of the world to be born without wings.
In the story, she ages from four to sixteen.

**In the darkness, as people take their seats, piano music starts, a vamp that plays
seemingly forever, all on the one rhythmic figure and in the one key – C-minor-seven
(the dominant) – so that, by the time we are ready for the first song much,
much later and we slide, at last, into F-minor-seven (the tonic), the feeling
of tension will have built up to the point where it will be a huge relief to be hearing,
finally, a different key. Not to mention an actual song. Anyway, in the dark,
the vamp is playing, the vamp is playing, the vamp is playing, playing, playing.
Suddenly, over it – and only when the auditorium is settled – a male voice
booms out on sound system (live or pre-recorded, director's choice).**

VOICE: From the dark.
Iskweewuk igwa naapeewuk, ladies and gentlemen, mesdames et messieurs, all the way from Petit Petit Le Paw, Manitoba, please welcome to the stage of the (name theatre and town), the one and only, the very talented, and the very beautiful, Miss Mary Jane Mosquito!

A light fades in. Off to stage right he sits at his grand piano, playing it; this is where the vamp is coming from. Otherwise, the stage is empty. The voice comes on again.

VOICE: From the dark.
Iskweewuk igwa naapeewuk, ladies and gentlemen, mesdames et messieurs, all the way from Petit Petit Le Paw, Manitoba, please welcome to the stage of the (name theatre and town), the one and only, the very talented, and the very beautiful, Miss Mary Jane Mosquito!

MARY JANE: From off-stage.
Coming!

VOICE: From off-stage, getting impatient.
Miss Mary Jane Mosquito!

Mary Jane Mosquito, a wingless little girl of four, comes running onstage fixing herself – her hair? her clothes? whatever – but stops when, to her amazement, she discovers that there is an audience sitting there watching her. The vamp on the piano stops. And in the dead silence, Mary Jane addresses the audience.

MARY JANE:
What are you doing here?

Pause. No answer.
You're not supposed to be here.

To pianist.
You didn't tell me they were here.

The pianist shrugs his shoulders – no response here either. So with immense trepidation, Mary Jane tries to start a conversation with the audience.
Ahm. Taansi, iskweewuk igwa naapeewuk... taan...si...

Awkward silence.
Ahm. That means...in my language, that means, "hello" or "greetings, ladies and gentlemen." Wanna learn how to say it? Try it. Taansi.

AUDIENCE:
Taansi.

MARY JANE:
See? It just means, "hello." Or "greetings." Anyway. Welcome to...my cabaret! This cabaret, of course – as you may know from the posters, the newspapers, the television, and the radio – is called, "The Incredible Adventures of Mary Jane Mosquito." Why? Because iskweewuk igwa naapeewuk – that means, "ladies and gentlemen" in my language – because I wanna share my story... with you. And you wanna know why I wanna share my story with you? Tell you a secret.

She whispers a huge stage whisper.
I don't have any friends. I don't know how to make friends.

Big pause. The vamp on the piano starts again. As if embarrassed, Mary Jane indicates the pianist.

Oh him. He's a...well...haven't you ever heard of an invisible friend? Like, a guardian angel? Someone who helps you out when you're in trouble? Or in pain? Well, that's what he is to me. Samba Cheese Sans-facon, rhymes with "telephone." Sam for short, he makes me sing. For God knows, singing is the only thing I know how to do. I'll show you.

Sings.
L'amour est en train d'entrer,
Dans...dans ma, dans ma,
Ma vie, ma vie;
L'amour, finalement,
Viens! Entrez, entrez, dans ma,
Ma vie.
L'amour est en train d'entrer,
Dans...dans mon, dans mon,
Mon coeur, mon coeur;
L'amour, finalement,
Viens! Entrez, entrez dans mon,
Mon coeur.

During the instrumental break that plays here, she speaks.
And because I'm here with you today, ladies and gentlemen, I'm sharing my song with you, which means I'm gonna share my life with you, right? Which means I'm gonna tell you about "the incredible adventures of Mary Jane Mosquito." So that's why I come all the way down here from Petit Petit Le Paw, northern Manitoba – by train – to beautiful (*name town and province – or state – or whatever*). To look for love, companionship, camaraderie, and friendship. That's what this song is about – love, companionship, friendship. And you know what? Ms. Mary Jane aims to find it right here in (*name town*). Cuz they say, legend has it... that (*name town*) is the best place in the whole wide world to find it, right, ladies and gentlemen? Don't the best friends to be found in the whole wide world live right here in this town, this burg, this fabulous, magic little city?

Sings.
Saageetoowin, saageetoowin
Nimoo, nimooseetaan, seetaan
Saageetoowin, saagee
Hey, astum, astum,
Peesaagee-in;
Saageetoowin, saageetoowin
Nimoo, nimooseetaan, seetaan
Saageetoowin, saagee
Hey, astum, astum,
Peesaagee-in;
Saageetoowin, saageetoowin

Music fades into silence. Mary Jane speaks.
Ah yes, love, friendship, company, that's what that song was about...

Silence. Complete change of rhythm. Suddenly, she speaks confidentially, intimately.
Ahem. When I was a young mosquito, that is, when I was first starting life out as a very, very young mosquito, life wasn't easy. No sir, it wasn't easy at all. You see, I didn't have a friend, didn't have a single...weecheewaagan. That means "friend" in my language. Weecheewaagan. Try it. Wee..

AUDIENCE:
Wee...

MARY JANE:
Chee...

AUDIENCE:
Chee...

MARY JANE:
Waagan.

AUDIENCE:
Waagan.

MARY JANE:
Weecheewaagan.

AUDIENCE:
Weecheewaagan.

MARY JANE:
Sounds like "wagon," don't it?
With a "weechee" in front of it.
Weecheewaagan. Means "friend."
Now point to yourself...

Points to self.
And say: "ni-weecheewaagan."

AUDIENCE:
Ni-weecheewaagan.

MARY JANE:
Very good. Means "my friend." One more time. Ni-weecheewaagan.

AUDIENCE:
Ni-weecheewaagan.

MARY JANE:
Now point to me and say...

Points to audience.
Ki-weecheewaagan.

AUDIENCE:
Ki-weecheewaagan.

MARY JANE:
Very good. Means, "your friend." One more time. Ki-weecheewaagan.

AUDIENCE:
Ki-weecheewaagan.

MARY JANE:
Very good. Now point to the neighbour on your right and say...

Points to her right using her thumb.
Oo-weecheewaagana.

AUDIENCE:
Oo-weecheewaagana.

MARY JANE:
Very good. Means "his friend" or "her friend" because, you see, there is no "he" or "she" in my language. One more time. Oo-weecheewaagana.

AUDIENCE:
Ooweecheewaagana.

MARY JANE:
Now combine all three. Say...

Makes appropriate hand gestures, her point being that they be copied by the audience.
Ni-weecheewaagan, ki-weecheewaagan, oo-weecheewaagana.

AUDIENCE:
Ni-weecheewaagan, ki-weecheewaagan, oo-weecheewaagana.

MARY JANE:
Ni-weecheewaagan, ki-weecheewaagan, oo-weecheewaagana.

AUDIENCE:
Ni-weecheewaagan, ki-weecheewaagan, oo-weecheewaagana.

MARY JANE:
Very good! Thank you, merci, igwaani kwayus, thank you. But anyway, when I was young, like you? I didn't have one of them. No sir, not a weecheewaagan in the whole wide world, none, maw keegway, zilch, pffft, boom! Why don't I have a friend? I used to ask myself. Everybody else in the world seems to have one, if not two or three. Even snobby, little, oopsy-doopsy, "oh, excusez-moi" Liza Jane Mosquito just down the street, has a friend. She has two, Anne-Marie Mosquito and Suzie Q. Mosquito, I used to say to myself as I would sit there on the steps of my mommy and my daddy's old brown porch, looking at the grass, looking at the flowers, looking at the chickadees singing in the trees, looking at the stars. All the mosquitoes in my town, Petit Petit Le Paw, Manitoba? They all had friends. They went to the store together, they went to the movies together, they went to the beach together. Why not me? I used to ask myself. Is it because I'm not...pretty? like Suzie Q. Mosquito with her cute blonde curls and her pointy little nose? Or is it because my legs are not long and lean and supple-as-a-willow like...like Elaine Victoria Mosquito's? And not only did they have friends, all these little girl mosquitoes, they had these beautiful...wings. And I didn't. I didn't have friends, I didn't have wings. All I had was these stupid little stubs on my shoulder blades, see? When would mine start growing? Why was I so slow? And they looked so...stupid, see? Why? Why didn't I have wings?

And she starts singing.

VERSE:
Somewhere a star,
Must surely think of me,
And pray that I,
Will not be lonely;
I dream about,
The day when someone new,
Will come my way,
And say, "I love you."

CHORUS:
But nights go by,
Days go by,
The hours go by,
And here am I,
I am who,
This lonely heart who'll always be one,
Never two.

*Here she does a dance, a small ballet
that expresses her loneliness and her
yearning for a friend.*

VERSE:
I need a friend,
Someone I can't forget,
Someone to call,
When I've a secret;
I long for a friend,
A friend to call upon,
When day is done,
And light is gone.

CHORUS.
CODA: Oh, somewhere a star…

Stop music. She speaks.

MARY JANE:
So they send me to school.
Kindergarten. I didn't wanna go.
But my parents said I'd make lots
of friends there. And I wanted to
believe them, oh, how I wanted to
believe them. So I did. Believe them.
Miss Kathleen B. Curdew's Centre
for the Education of Very Young
Mosquitoes, right there in downtown
Petit Petit Le Paw, Manitoba which,
you must understand, is not very
big to begin with. You see, there's
Le Paw, Manitoba proper. Then
there's Petit Le Paw, Manitoba. Then
there's Petit Petit Le Paw and that's
where I'm from and that's where
Miss Kathleen B. Curdew's Centre
for the Education of Very Young
Mosquitoes is located. Except...
Miss Kathleen B. Curdew herself
was actually...dead. So she didn't
teach there. But you know who did?
Her daughter, Maggie May Curdew-
slash-Ditchburn. Yes, Maggie May
Ditchburn, taller than a ladder, taller
than a tree, tall as...the CN Tower.

She gulps.
I remember that first time I saw her. She had eyes like...like a...a swooping hawk. And she looks down at me. And she says to me, as I'm standing there right in front of all the other four-year-old mosquitoes – 1,500 of them! – and she says to me, "Mary Jane Mosquito, my, my. How very interesting. Don't you think that's interesting, class?"

Mary Jane Mosquito

She almost cries but then rallies.
I wanted to curl up into a ball and disappear because I knew she was talking about my... well, I just looked funny. I mean, a mosquito without wings, that's like a dog with no tail. Or a...or a...a man with no legs. I wanna sing to myself so I won't have to hear her voice but then she says, Miss Maggie May says, as if she'd just read my mind, "Let's all sing a song together, class." It was horrible. And that wasn't the only time. At least once a week, Miss Maggie May would put us in a line and she'd make us stand up stiff, tall, like statues in a park, straight neck, straight back, straight legs, wings out like...like...like kites in the wind. Well, those of us who had wings cuz I sure didn't. Yet. And she'd make us march in the schoolyard, like wind-up toy soldiers. Hup, two, three, four. Hup, two, three, four. "Nagamoon." That was the title of the song Miss Maggie Curdew-slash-Ditchburn used to make us sing. Nagamoon. Say it. Nagamoon.

Hup two three four

AUDIENCE:
Nagamoon.

MARY JANE:
Thank you. Means "song" in the language of mosquitoes.
Nagamooon, nagamoon, nagamoon.

AUDIENCE:
Nagamooon, nagamoon, nagamoon.

MARY JANE:
Nagamooon, nagamoon, nagamoon.

AUDIENCE:
Nagamooon, nagamoon, nagamoon.

MARY JANE:
Now point to yourself like this and say: ni-nagamoon.

AUDIENCE:
Ni-nagamoon.

MARY JANE:
Thank you. That means, "my song." One more
time. Ni-nagamoon.

AUDIENCE:
Ni-nagamoon.

MARY JANE:
Very good. Thank you. Now point to me
and say: ki-nagamoon.

AUDIENCE:
Ki-nagamoon.

MARY JANE:
Thank you. That means "your song." One more
time. Ki-nagamoon.

AUDIENCE:
Ki-nagamoon.

MARY JANE:
Very good. Thank you. Now all three, one after the other after the other. Repeat after me.

She uses all the appropriate hand gestures.
Ni-nagamoon, ki-nagamoon, oo-nagamoon.

AUDIENCE:
Like Mary Jane, they use all the appropriate hand gestures.
Ni-nagamoon, ki-nagamoon, oo-nagamoon.

MARY JANE:
Ain't that purty? Means "my song, your song, his/her song." One more time. Ni-nagamoon, ki-nagamoon, oo-nagamoon.

AUDIENCE:
Ni-nagamoon, ki-nagamoon, oo-nagamoon.

MARY JANE:
Ni-nagamoon, ki-nagamoon, oo-nagamoon.

AUDIENCE:
Ni-nagamoon, ki-nagamoon, oo-nagamoon.

MARY JANE:
Now try this. Hup, ni-nagamoon, ki-nagamoon, oo-nagamoon. Hup, ni-nagamoon, ki-nagamoon, oo-nagamoon. Join me. We'll do it together, three, four...

AUDIENCE/MARY JANE:
Hup, ni-nagamoon, ki-nagamoon, oo-nagamoon.
Hup, ni-nagamoon, ki-nagamoon, oo-nagamoon.
Hup, ni-nagamoon, ki-nagamoon, oo-nagamoon.
Hup...

The audience keeps up the pattern for as long as it can for they will fade away in increments, in any case, as Mary Jane's song progresses.

So the other little bugs would a-giggle and a-roar,
So the other little critters would a-titter to the core,
At Mary Jane's expense, yes, at *my* expense,
She was jealous, she was jealous, I'm not dense,
Miss Maggie May Ditchburn was as jealous as a ver*mine*,
Jealous as a snake and as jealous as a swine,
Cuz deep down in her heart, in her tired old heart,
She knew I had a future she couldn't dream a wart,
She knew I could become, knew I *would* become,
Everything she'd dreamt of, everything and some,
But she never would attain, never would become,
Like sing on all the stages of kingdom come,
Like fly down to the south for a real fine tan,
Like buy a little nest in Man-hat-tan,

She was jealous, she
was jealous and I well
knew it,
    She was out to get *la moi*,
and more than just a bit,
    Can you imagine anything
so foolish, so unwise?
    "So Mary Jane Mosquito, I
strongly you advise,
    Soon as you can do it, a-quicker
than a deer,
    Grab yourself a bag and get on out of
here,
    Fly away from here, leave Petit Petit,
    Yes, fly away from here and leave it
with a bee."
I'm saying to myself as I'm marching in the line,
I'm saying to myself in this little
heart of mine,
As Maggie May Ditchburn is
a-bangin' on her kitty,
And I'm a-singin' and
a-howlin' and
a-wailin' right
along,
Miss Maggie
May Ditchburn's
simple little ditty,
Miss Maggie
May Ditchburn's
simple little song,
Hup, two, three,
four,
    Hup, two three, four.

    Patty cake, patty cake, baker man,
    Bake me a cake a-faster than you can,
    Tommy-let, tommy-let, take your pan,
    Make me an ommy-let that's bigger
    than a man,
        Daddy cake, daddy cake, take
        your van,

Take me to the beach
for a real fine tan,
Mary Jane, Mary Jane,
daughter of the man,
Give me any lip and I'll
put you in a can.

Patty cake, patty cake
paagweesiganis,
Paagweesiganis and
paagweesiganis,
Tommy-let, tommy-let saasapiskisa,
Saasapiskisa and saasapiskisa,
Daddy cake, daddy cake, ootaapaanaas ootin,
Ootaapaanaas ootin and ootaapaanaas ootin,
Mary Jane, Mary Jane pooninagamoo,
Pooninagamoo and pooninagamoo.

Patty cake, patty cake, baker man,
Bake me a cake a-faster than you can,
Tommy-let, tommy-let, take your pan,
Make me an ommy-let that's bigger than a man,
Daddy cake, daddy cake, take your van,
 Take me to the beach for a real fine tan,
 Mary Jane, Mary Jane, daughter of the man,
 Give me any lip and I'll put you in a can.

Patty cake, patty cake paagweesiganis,
Paagweesiganis and paagweesiganis,
Tommy-let, tommy-let saasapiskisa,
Saasapiskisa and saasapiskisa,
Daddy cake, daddy cake, ootaapaanaas ootin,
Ootaapaanaas ootin and ootaapaanaas ootin,
Mary Jane, Mary Jane pooninagamoo,
Pooninagamoo and pooninagamoo.

Except...except I was the only mosquito there. The rest? House flies, horse flies, black flies, deer flies, sand flies, dragon flies, every kind of fly you could imagine, even some from Nunavut, bees, hornets, wasps – the wasps? Oh, they were the worst! – black moths, white moths, big moths, small moths, butterflies from Mexico, even tsetse flies from far Nigeria. But neither a stitch nor a hair nor a squiggle of an itsy bitsy teeny weeny sweet mosquito. Just...moi. Old Aunt Flo told me they sent mosquitoes to a school in the south of the city because they made too much trouble but she lived in the north and Winnipeg's a big city and...well...I would have had to take a bus one hour every day each way, all by myself. At age seven years? Impossible. She wouldn't let me do that. So I just had to suffer the consequences. So here I am the only mosquito in the whole wide world, far as I'm concerned. And lonely? Oh my God, I was lonely. I'd lie there in my bed at old Aunt Flo's feeling the little wing stubs on my shoulder blades. Trying to look at them in

Matouche, will you be my friend?" "No," says Minnie Matouche, flicks out her wings, and just flies away. Leaving me standing in the middle of the schoolyard looking like a fool, a fool for love. Well, that was it. First I heard laughter somewhere behind me. Then I heard a roar somewhere in my head. Then I saw red. A deep blood red. And then...I don't know how I did it, if I jumped up to catch her when she dared to buzz me or what, but I attacked her. I attacked Minnie Matouche, that terrible mouche, in a way no housefly has ever, *ever* been attacked before.

She uses a squeaky little munchkin voice to mimic her tormentors.

"Tee-hee, tee-hee, mosquito, tee-hee..." Mean, huh? Then one day I combed my hair, straightened out my dress, steeled my nerves, and I went up to this girl, a chubby little housefly with a freckly little nose named, of all things, Minnie...Matouche...if you can believe such a thing. Now what kind of a name is that for a housefly, I thought to myself, for you see, in French? a housefly is called a "mouche." La mouche, Minnie Matouche, get it? I wanted to burst out laughing right then and there but I kept my cool for you see, for once, I thought I might have a chance with...*her*. So I walk up to Minnie, real cool, and I say: "Say there, Minnie

Instrumental break here where we get to see Ms. Mosquito have a terrible tussle with the invisible Minnie Matouche. At one point during her "dance," she snarls out these words at the audience:

Wanna see what an angry mosquito looks like?

Then she goes back to her spoken song.
So I said to her there, "Don't you dare!"
Come one step more and I'll tell your mère!"
So you know what she does, that terrible
  mouche?
She tore from her sack a tin can of mush;

"RAID!" they call it, it sprays with a gush?
At which point there came this terrible hush,
At which point I yelled, "Minnie Matouche?
Come over here and I'll give you a woosh!"

At which point she fainted, right there
  in the middle,
Hey, diddly-doo, the cat and the fiddle,
And that was my fight with Minnie Matouche,
With Minnie Matouche, the terrible mouche;

"RAID!" they call it, it sprays with a gush?
At which point there came this terrible hush,
At which point I yelled, "Minnie Matouche?
Come over here and I'll give you a woosh!"

At which point she fainted, right there
  in the middle,
Hey, diddly-doo, the cat and the fiddle,
And that was my fight with Minnie Matouche,
With Minnie Matouche, the terrible mouche;

She fainted, she fainted right there in the middle,
Hey, diddly-doo, the cat and the fiddle,
And that was my fight with Minnie Matouche,
With Minnie Matouche, the terrible mouch;

And that was my fight with Minnie Matouche,
With Minnie Matouche, the terrible mouche,
With Minnie Matouche, the terrible mouche,
With Minnie Matouche, the terrible mouche,

With Minnie la la la la
  la la la la la la la la la
  la la la la la
  La la la la la la la la
  la la la la
  mooooooooooooooooooosh!

*End music. She catches her breath,
straightens herself out, then resumes
talking to the audience...even
though she has to
gasp for breath.*

Ahem. Needless to say, I still had no friends. I walked home that day, sent home early for what the principal called "my disgraceful behaviour." And it *was* disgraceful. But I didn't want to fight. It just happened. That's not what I wanted to be, this ugly mean little thing. I didn't hate Minnie Matouche. I didn't hate any of those flies. If I hated anyone now, it was me. Yes, I hated myself, hated myself so much I wanted to...well, never mind. So what was I to do to...to change all that? I get home. And my old Aunt Flo, she's cleaning up my scratches, my bumps, my bruises. I was so scared. I was sure she'd get mad and punish me. I look up at her face. And it was so kind. And she says to me...

Piano music starts at about here, a gentle waltz, over which Mary Jane continues speaking.

"Mary Jane, my niece? You know what your problem is? "What?" I say. And she says, "You don't trust yourself. You don't love yourself. And therefore you don't let others trust you or love you. You can't just expect to go out and take. You have to learn to give. Because you see, when you show ten times the kindness, to others, sooner or later, it will come back to you, ten times ten times ten..."

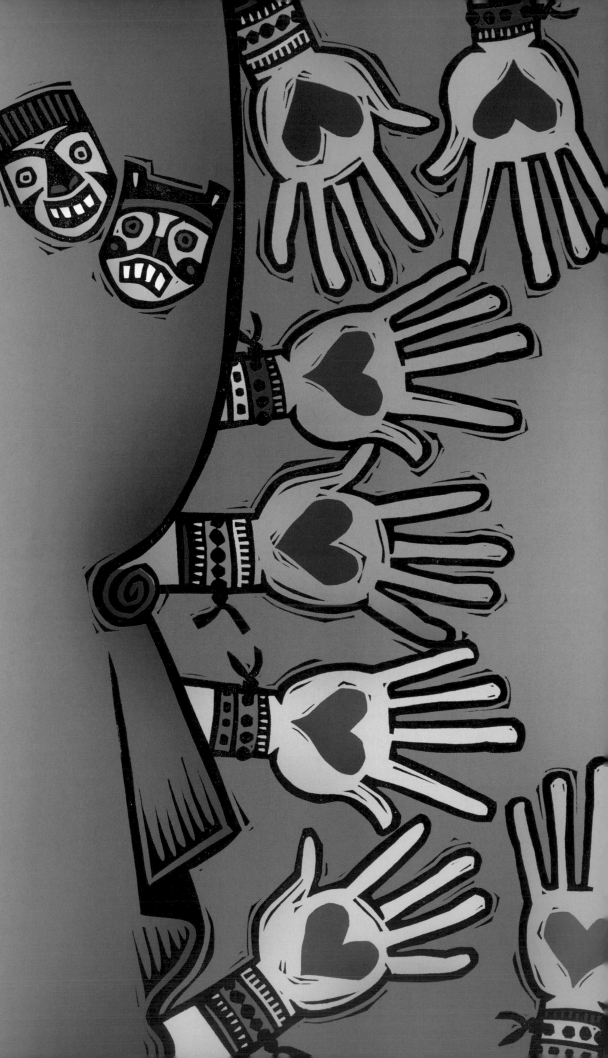

And Mary Jane starts singing.
Ten times ten times, that's how it works,
Ten times ten times, you'll see it works,
Love sent, love given, comes back to you,
Love felt, love shared, it comes back to you.

*As an instrumental break goes on
under her voice, she resumes speaking.*
That's what she says. Then she says to
me, "Maybe you should go somewhere
where friends are to be had. They say
there is such a place, you know, out east
(or out west or down south or whatever),
a town called (name town the show is
playing in). Tell me, Mary Jane, if you were
to go to a place like that, what would you
give? What *could* you give to the people of
(name town)? "I don't know," I said. She
looks at me. "Guess." And then I say, "Do
you think I'll ever get wings?" And she says,
"That will come. Just let Mother Nature
have her way. You'll see. Just be kind...give
them your gift. Without expecting anything
in return." She nods. And it all comes to
me – song, my singing, that's my gift, that's
what I can give...

52

And she sings.
Ten times ten times, that's
   how it works,
Ten times ten times, you'll see
   it works,
Love sent, love given, comes
   back to you,
Love felt, love shared, it comes
   back to you.

And again, as an instrumental break goes on under her voice, she resumes, speaks.

Ah yes, ten times ten times ten times ten... She drove me to the train station, old Aunt Flo. Put some money in my pocket, kissed me goodbye, put me on the train, cried a little bit, and waved goodbye with her crumpled, tear-stained, little white cotton handkerchief. And now I'm on the train, travelling east, east through Manitoba and into Ontario (make adjustments as to the route to be travelled). The trees were so beautiful, the lakes, the rivers, I even saw a bear...thinking...in the woods...and I waved at him and he waved back and he was so happy and I was so happy and...I'm sitting there looking out the window, looking at the chickadees singing in the trees. And me, too, I'm singing and singing and singing and singing. Sing with me!

And the audience joins her for the final chorus.

AUDIENCE/MARY JANE:
Ten times ten times, that's how it works,
Ten times ten times, you'll see it works,
Love sent, love given, comes back to you,
Love felt, love shared, it comes back to you.

CODA:
Love felt, love shared, it comes back to you,
Love felt, love shared, it comes back to you.

End music for this song, start music for the next.
And Mary Jane goes back to speaking.

MARY JANE:
Thank you, iskweewuk igwa naapeewuk, ladies and
gentlemen, thank you, thank you, thank you, igwaani
kwayus, thank you.

With huge joy and enthusiasm, she goes into the audience and shakes this hand and that hand and this hand and that hand, addressing each person as she goes along. All along, the introduction to the last song in the show plays under her voice – it is actually the endless vamp from the top of the show, perfect for a walk through the audience.

Mary Jane Mosquito, nice to meet you. What's your name? David? Awesome. Mary Jane Mosquito, treat to meet you. What's your name? Amber? Sweet. Mary Jane Mosquito, an honour to meet you. Your name? Brad? Cool. Mary Jane Mosquito, nice to meet you. Your name? Jasmine? Gorgeous. Mary Jane Mosquito, big thrill to meet you. Your name? Cowboy?! Holy! Etc... (room for improvisation here...).

Until she starts making her way back to the stage.

So now, Mary Jane Mosquito, she has no fear. Now she makes her way through the streets of this town and the streets of that town and the streets of this city and the streets of that city and this and that and this and that and this, that, and whatsit meeting people here and meeting people there and greeting people here and greeting people there and making friends left, right, and all over the place because, it's true, I don't need wings to fly. I can fly on my own just fine, thank you, in my heart. It's not what you look like that matters, Aunt Flo's words ring in my ears like chimes in the wind, it's what you give to others that counts. Mother Nature can take all the time she wants with my wings. I don't need them. I have you. And you and you and you. And you and you and you. And you there in the bright red T-shirt and you there with the long black hair and you there with the big brown eyes. Friends for life, right? Right.

*And she breaks
into song.*

Saageetoowin,
  saageetoowin
Nimoo, nimooseetaan,
  seetaan
Saageetoowin, saagee
Hey, astum, astum,
Peesaagee-in;
L'amour est en train
  d'entrer,
Dans...dans ma, dans
  ma vie,
Ma vie, ma vie;
L'amour, finalement,
Viens! Entrez, entrez
  dans ma,
Ma vie.

*For the last instrumental break, she introduces her pianist
who keeps playing uninterrupted.*
Iskweewuk igwa naapeewuk, ladies igwa gentlemen, my guardian
angel, Samba San-façon, rhymes with "telephone."

*And he launches into a flashy little solo. Following which Mary Jane
sings and speaks the coda to the song, which is simply...*

Saagee,,,

Speaks.
That means "love."

Sings.
Toowin...

Speaks.
In my language...

Sings.
Saagee,,,

Speaks.
"Love..."

Sings.
Toowin...

Speaks.
"Love..."

*She freezes, lights fade to black,
end music in the dark.*

THE END.